Acting Edition

Off Off Broadway Festival Plays, 47th Series

Chemistry
by Ben Holbrook

Bugs
by Alex Moon

If All That You Take From This Is Courage, Then I've No Regrets
by Nicholas Pilapil

Shark Week
by Erika Phoebus

Georgia Rose
by Onyekachi Iwu

Too Much Lesbian Drama: One Star
by Jessie Field

‖SAMUEL FRENCH‖

ISBN 978-0-573-71026-1

www.concordtheatricals.com
www.concordtheatricals.co.uk

FOR PRODUCTION INQUIRIES

UNITED STATES AND CANADA
info@concordtheatricals.com
1-866-979-0447

UNITED KINGDOM AND EUROPE
licensing@concordtheatricals.co.uk
020-7054-7298

Each title is subject to availability from Concord Theatricals Corp.,
depending upon country of performance. Please be aware that *OFF
OFF BROADWAY FESTIVAL PLAYS, 47TH SERIES* may not be
licensed by Concord Theatricals Corp. in your territory. Professional
and amateur producers should contact the nearest Concord Theatricals
Corp. office or licensing partner to verify availability.

---

starting rehearsals, advertising, or booking a theatre. A licensing fee must be paid whether the title(s) is presented for charity or gain and whether or not admission is charged. Professional/Stock licensing fees are quoted upon application to Concord Theatricals Corp.

This work is published by Samuel French, an imprint of Concord Theatricals Corp.

For all inquiries regarding motion picture, television, online/digital and other media rights, please contact Concord Theatricals Corp.

MUSIC AND THIRD-PARTY MATERIALS USE NOTE

Licensees are solely responsible for obtaining formal written permission from copyright owners to use copyrighted music and/or other copyrighted third-party materials (e.g. artworks, logos) in the performance of this play and are strongly cautioned to do so. If no such permission is obtained by the licensee, then the licensee must use only original music and materials that the licensee owns and controls. Licensees are solely responsible and liable for clearances of all third-party copyrighted materials, including without limitation music, and shall indemnify the copyright owners of the play(s) and their licensing agent, Concord Theatricals Corp., against any costs, expenses, losses and liabilities arising from the use of such copyrighted third-party materials by licensees. For music, please contact the appropriate music licensing authority in your territory for the rights to any incidental music.

IMPORTANT BILLING AND CREDIT REQUIREMENTS

If you have obtained performance rights to this title, please refer to your licensing agreement for important billing and credit requirements.

Concord Theatricals presents The Samuel French Off Off Broadway Short Play Festival (OOB) has been the nation's leading short play festival for forty-seven years. The OOB Festival has served as a doorway to future success for aspiring writers. Over two hundred plays have been published, and many participants have become established, award-winning playwrights.

For more information on the Off Off Broadway Short Play Festival, including history, interviews, and more, please visit www.oobfestival.com.

Festival Sponsor: Concord Theatricals

Festival Artistic Director: Casey McLain
Literary Manager: Garrett Anderson
Festival Host/Client Manager: Abbie Van Nostrand
Opening Night Party Moderator: Amy Rose Marsh
Box Office Manager: Rosemary Bucher
Production Stage Manager: Billie Davis
COVID-19 Compliance Officer: Rachel Levens
Marketing Team: Jeremiah Hernandez, Courtney Kochuba, Imogen Lloyd Webber, Rosalind Jackson Roe, Michael Valladares
Festival Production Coordinator: Grace Cutler

Festival Staff/Readers: : Alex Perez, Ally Varitek, Cara Kramer, Caroline Barnard, Charlie Coulthard, Elizabeth Minski, Ella Andrew, Fiona Kyle, Gabriela Morales, Kristen Rea, Meg Schadl, Nate Netzley, Oli Gordon, Rachel Smith, Sarah Weber, Sean Demers, Sequoyah Douglas, Tyler Mullen, William Whitaker, Stephanie Jane Cerino

HONORARY GUEST PLAYWRIGHT
Joshua Harmon

FESTIVAL JUDGES
Dennis A. Allen II
Nan Barnett
Eboni Booth
Ken Cerniglia
Karen Hartman
Margaret M. Ledford
Emily Morse
Jill Rafson
Natasha Sinha
Bryna Turner
Alexis Williams
Emmanuel Wilson

TABLE OF CONTENTS

FOREWORD

Concord Theatricals is honored to have the six daring and inspirational playwrights included in this collection as the winners of our 47th Annual Off Off Broadway Short Play Festival. This year our Festival received over seven hundred and fifty submissions from around the world. We thank all of these gifted playwrights for sharing their talent with us and welcome each writer into our elite group of Off Off Broadway Festival winners.

This year was our first in-person Festival in three years, and we were excited and nervous to be back at it. We started out a bit timid, unsure if it was too soon to be back in-person. However, it was just like riding a bike – and when we heard the audience cheer and applaud for the first performance, we knew we were in the right place at the right time. It was truly an honor to spend the week in the theatre with the Top-Thirty amazing plays and playwrights.

From our initial pool of Top-Thirty playwrights, we ultimately select six plays for publication and representation by Concord Theatricals. Of course, we can't make our selections alone, so we enlist some brilliant minds within the theatre industry to help us in this process. We invited an esteemed group of nine judges consisting of a mix of Concord Theatricals playwrights and members of the theatre industry. We thank them for their support, insight, and commitment to the art of playwriting.

Concord Theatricals is the world's most significant theatrical company, comprising the catalogs of R&H Theatricals, Samuel French, Tams-Witmark, and The Andrew Lloyd Webber Collection. We are constantly striving to develop groundbreaking methods that will better connect playwright and producer. With a team committed to continuing our tradition of publishing and licensing the best new theatrical works, we are boldly embracing our role in this industry as bridge between playwright and theatre.

On behalf of the entire Concord Theatricals team in our New York, London, and Berlin offices, and the over ten thousand playwrights, composers, and lyricists that we publish and represent, we present you with the six winning plays of the 47th Annual Samuel French Off Off Broadway Short Play Festival.

This festival is about playwrights. Sharing the human story. We invite you to enjoy these extraordinary plays.

Casey McLain
Artistic Director
The Samuel French Off Off Broadway Short Play Festival

Chemistry

A Vibe in One Act

Ben Holbrook

CHEMISTRY was originally produced by The Motor Company and directed by Phoebe Padget as a part of Laundryfest 2018. The cast was as follows:

THAD..Jamaal Anthony

JOJO...Jarielle Whitney

CHEMISTRY was also produced by the 47th Annual Off Off Broadway Short Play Festival in August 2022. The performance was directed by James Blaszko. The cast was as follows:

THAD.. Kemari Bryant

JOJO..Chandler Gregoir

CHARACTERS

THAD
JOJO

ACT ONE

Scene One

(**THAD** *sits on a bench in the laundromat, waiting for his clothes to dry. He has headphones on and does the crossword, while he eats Starbursts from a pack in his pocket.* **JOJO** *enters. She takes a breath, building up her courage to speak to* **THAD**.)

JOJO. Hey Pete, I've got a message for you from Ollie, he says, uh, you ain't nobody. That he can't believe how you could use him like that. Get his hopes up and then –

(**THAD**, *who hasn't reacted at all, looks up for the first time. He slowly begins to comprehend that* **JOJO** *may be speaking to him.*)

– get him to open up like that. He told you everything. Things he never told anybody. He really felt –

(**THAD** *takes his headphones off.*)

THAD. Are you talking to me?

JOJO. Huh?

THAD. I can't tell. You're talking to me, right?

JOJO. Yeah! I'm giving you a message.

THAD. Oh, cause I didn't hear any of that.

JOJO. None of it?

THAD. Not even a little bit, what kind of message? What's it about?

JOJO. This is a message from –

THAD. It's not about Jesus or/ something, is it?

JOJO. /What? Jesus? I don't know Jesus like that, that would be so weird.

THAD. Oh okay, so this is an actual thing? I don't have any money,/ just so you know.

JOJO. /No, it's not like that, I'm not/ Plus you're in a laundromat, if I was looking for change this place would be perfect, but I'm not.

THAD. /Oh okay, sorry. You never know!

JOJO. Can I just give you/ the message?

THAD. Yeah, sorry. This is kind of neat, I never get messages. It's like a telegram.

JOJO. Okay. Ready? Okay. Ollie up the street says that he can't believe how you used him like that. You got his hopes up, getting him to open up like that. He told you everything! Things he never told anybody. He felt like, for the first time, he could really be his self with someone. Just the two of you, side by side, being unapologetically real. He even started seeing a future with you, 'cause every time he'd think of you, his heart would fill with light. He came out to his mom and everything! Do you know how hard that was? And then you just went and disappeared like that? You left him to deal with all of this alone. He gave you the most personal, deepest parts of him and you just ran away with them. Gone. He's incomplete now and he'll never ever love, or connect with anybody like that ever again, 'cause you ruined him with your soft boy antics and he wants you to know that you're nothin'. A void, or...hold on.

THAD. Yeah, we should take a break, this is intense.

JOJO. Right?? When I heard it for the first time I was like "Daaaaamn, for real?? Homeboy was so reckless with your heart!"

THAD. Same here! He just disappeared?? Where did he go? Did he just fall out of contact? Maybe something happened. Do you have a picture of Ollie?

JOJO. Why would I?

THAD. I want to see what he looks like.

JOJO. What're you talkin' about? You know him, you broke his heart!

THAD. I'm sorry, I definitely didn't.

JOJO. He came out to his mom and everything!

THAD. That is so crazy! This was his first love?

JOJO. You ain't Pete?

THAD. Hell no. My name's Thad and I'm so, so glad that I'm not Pete, but this is some juicy stuff. Also, did you memorize that,/ Or are you paraphrasing?

JOJO. /Yeah. I memorized it.

THAD. That's crazy!

JOJO. I'm good at memorizin' stuff. Especially stuff I like, but sometimes people pay me to remember things.

THAD. Ollie paid you to recite that?

JOJO. Yeah, but now I have to give him a refund, cause you ain't Pete and I just wasted like four minutes delivering a message to you and I need that fifteen dollars cause my little cousin has prom coming up and I wanna help her get a dress and it's like "damn", you know?

THAD. Prom dresses can get expensive.

JOJO. Yeah and my aunt just can't do it right now, so I'm over here like "I gotchu", but they're all like "you ain't shit Jojo".

THAD. They don't have to be rude about it. You let them say stuff like that to you?

JOJO. I don't have a reputation for being the most reliable person in the family, but I've been pretty good delivering these messages. Nobody wants to pay a lot, though.

THAD. Yeah, you're competing with text messages.

JOJO. I know, but some things are better said in person. By a person. By me.

THAD. Like coming out to your mom.

JOJO. Yeah. Oh! One guy asked me to tell the dudes at the bodega that he asked for no tomato on his sandwich, but the bodega guy put it on anyway. So this dude had me memorize a whole lecture on the importance of listening and then a rant about how angry he was and how he took it off but the juice from the tomato was still on everything and made him gag after every bite. That one was a ten-dollar one. I get a lot of stuff like that.

THAD. You should've charged more. That kind of sounds fun though.

JOJO. Oh no. It ain't.

THAD. But you get to know everybody's/ business.

JOJO. It's all too personal. I'm, like, carrying people's personal shit. I don't really like memorizing people's pain. Nobody's given me a good message like a "thank you" or a "I miss you". It's all shit that somebody wants, or needs from somebody else, or things people want each other to feel bad for and they're scared to say it in person, or just won't.

THAD. So what would you rather memorize?

JOJO. I like chemicals.

THAD. Huh?

JOJO. Well not *like*, like, but they stick.

THAD. You're fascinated by them?

JOJO. Yeah, like, you use Tide?

THAD. Yeah.

JOJO. Laundry detergent is crazy, you can see all the chemicals on the side like sodium hydroxide and borax and ethanolamine, but there's at least seventeen in there that ain't listed.

THAD. That should be illegal, is that illegal?

JOJO. I don't know, but a lot of them are byproducts of creating the Tide. Like, you mix two chemicals and sometimes they bond and create another one, like 1,4-dioxane, which is in varnishes and stuff, but shouldn't be on your skin cause it messes with your brain toxicity and nervous system and liver and kidneys. Long term exposure can mess you up, it can't be washed out in rinse cycle, either so it stays on your clothes and when you sweat your skin absorbs it.

(*Pause.*)

THAD. That reminds me of my last relationship. Two normal people get together and somehow that bond created something toxic.

JOJO. Ohhh! That's deep!

(**THAD** *shrugs.*)

THAD. It's crazy how it happens. It's like, "Hey you're cool, you're nice, you like good music, I'm the same, let's do this!" But there's just something that doesn't work or can't work, you may not even know what it is, like a curse, or something. Energy just gets all messed up and... I don't know, some chemicals don't mix.

JOJO. Oh! It's like medicine! Like digoxin.

THAD. A chemical?

JOJO. C-41 H-64 O-14! it's supposed to treat stuff dealing with the heart. Like increase its efficiency if you have heart problems. But some research shows that patients on it had a thirty-five percent increase in cardiovascular-related deaths.

THAD. Yeah, that's it. You thought they'd be good for your heart, but they just made it worse.

JOJO. People depend on chemicals too much. Like, some are good for you and really do help, but a lot of them are rough.

THAD. What about you?

JOJO. There was a doctor that admitted to killing like forty people using digoxin.

THAD. Whoa! I don't even think I'm ready to – weren't we talkin' about love? Let's talk about that chemical.

JOJO. Norepinephrine, makes your heart race and your palms sweat, Dopamine, makes you feel pleasure, phenylethylamine, is the releasing agents for those first two. Those are the love chemicals.

THAD. So is there anyone out there that gets your phenylteh-amacallit going?

JOJO. Phenylethylamine? Nah. I don't really do that stuff.

THAD. No?

JOJO. I don't like guys.

THAD. Girls?

JOJO. No. They smell better, but I don't really like any of that stuff. It's weird and heavy and I honestly don't get it. Like, don't get me wrong, I love a good cuddle with somebody that's soft and warm. That's so, so nice.

THAD. But nothing else?

JOJO. I mean, making out is okay, but sometimes it just makes me uncomfortable.

THAD. Wow...I kind of envy you. I feel like I spend so much time trying to make out. Like sixty percent of my time. It would be nice to just not care.

JOJO. Nah. You say that, but like, people put so much into love and relationships. Like, every song is about it. Nobody sings about cuddling. There's no Boyz II Men song about cuddling "till the water runs dry" or an Usher song that's like "I just wanna cuddle nice and slow." There's no song that's like, oo let me cuddle with you, oo let me cuddle –

THAD. Ayy! Let me cuddle with you, oo, let me cuddle!

JOJO. Hey, I'm tryin' to cuddle with you, too, let me cuddle!

THAD & JOJO. Oo let me cuddle with you, oo let me cuddle!

THAD. *(Singing.[1])*
I'M TRYIN' TO CUDDLE WITH YOU TILL' THE SUNRISE,
IN THE SUNLIGHT, GET IN OUR PAJAMAS AND –

No, no let me stop, before we end up on billboard.

JOJO. Like, I'm the only person I know who *actually* wants to Netflix and chill and is totally satisfied doing just that. I like the way I am just fine, but a lot of people don't get it. They think I'm broken.

THAD. You know that you're not though, right?

JOJO. Yeah! I know! Don't tell me, tell them!

---

1. A license to produce *Chemistry* does not include a performance license for any third-party or copyrighted music. Licensees should create an original composition or use music in the public domain. For further information, please see the Music and Third-Party Materials Use Note on page iii.

THAD. Well, sounds to me like your heart works fine, since you're spending all of your time trying to get your niece this prom dress. How much do you need?

JOJO. Huh?

THAD. For the dress?

JOJO. Twenty-five dollars more. That reminds me, I have to deliver another –

THAD. I have a message for you.

JOJO. Oh shit, okay! Wassup? What is it?

THAD. It's for Ollie.

JOJO. I knew you were Pete!

THAD. Seriously, I'm not, I swear!

JOJO. You're so Pete!

THAD. For real, I'm not!

JOJO. Fine, what is it?

THAD. Um, okay. Wait...Okay I'm ready. Hey Ollie, Pete wasn't here, but my name is Thad. I heard your message and I just wanted to say that what Pete did was...messed up and I feel your pain and your heartache. I remember the first time I was in love with someone like, for real, and they couldn't handle it. I wanted to give them everything, but they couldn't hold all of that. Sometimes people tell you they want all of you and don't realize that you're a whole human, with a whole personality and past, and it may never dawn on them that they asked you to give them something that people have no right to have. Walking around with other people's pain is hard.

JOJO. Preach.

THAD. And most people aren't strong enough, or enlightened enough to do it. Not like Jojo. I hope that

Pete comes back. I hope that Pete apologizes and you two cry for hours and feel better after and can be friends and trust each other and cuddle until the sunrise.

JOJO. *"In the sunlight!"* Yes, please!

THAD. But I hope, more than any of that, that you can let yourself love again and that you hold your own past and your own pain and learn to love and accept all of it, because you're not Pete's, you're not your mom's, you're yours. You're your own experience. You're more than love, you're kindness and sensitivity and hope. You're everything. So don't let someone else's shortcomings hold you back from being the full, beautiful thing you are. I hope that coming out to your mom went okay, I hate that sometimes parents don't get it, it's like damn, if you're not prepared to love an entire human being for who they are no matter what, then don't make one, but that's just me and you seem like a really brave guy, who loves with all of his heart, so I'd be proud of you. I am proud of you. If it's rocky, give it time, sometimes these things smooth out. If you want to talk, I'll be at the laundromat for fifteen more minutes, waiting for my stuff to dry and finishing this crossword. Okay, that's it.

JOJO. I really like that. That was a really good message. I'll do that one for free.

THAD. Free?? That was a lot!

JOJO. It's easy though. And you said you didn't have any money...

THAD. I just remembered that I had enough for a tip.

> (**THAD** *gives* **JOJO** *twenty-five dollars, she counts it.*)

JOJO. Really?? Oh, can I hug you??

THAD. Please. *(They hug. They enjoy it.)*

JOJO. *(Still hugging him.)* For real though, stop using Tide.

THAD. Okay.

JOJO. *(Releasing him.)* Okay, I gotta job to do!

(**JOJO** *exits.*)

Bugs

Alex Moon

BUGS received a staged reading in 2022 through the 47th Annual Off Off Broadway Short Play Festival under the direction of Kelsey Sullivan. The cast was as follows:

THIERRY . . . . Grace Santos

BRUCE . . . . Amanda Morrow

BUG . . . . Jordan Jackson

CHARACTERS

THIERRY – Thirty to fifty, male

BRUCE – Thirty to fifty, male

BUGS – Played by humans. Don't need to remotely look like bugs. The shittier the better.

SETTING

Somewhere along I-80 in Iowa.

TIME

The Present. Sunset.

AUTHOR'S NOTES

*A "/ " indicates overlapping dialogue.

**A NOTE ON TONE:

During a reading of this piece, one collaborator remarked that this play felt like "The Call of the Void" – That feeling you get when you're driving alone at night and you find your mind wandering to the liminal, fearful, and unknown; Where a voice that's not your own wonders what would happen if you just let go of the wheel...

Or maybe that's just me.

Point is, I found that statement described the nature of this play far better than anything I could say about it, and with that understanding, a few things should be mentioned. This play is a comedy with a dark, tragic center. The pace should be snappy. Both Bruce and Thierry should be equally loveable in their care for each other. Bruce's moment alone should not be overly-alluded to, but rather comes as a sharp break from the tone established at top of show. Thierry's return marks a convergence and hopefully a reconciliation of these two tones.

(A deserted stretch of highway. Early evening. **BUG**, *with a lackluster pair of antennae, smokes a cigarette, morose, forlorn.)*

(Lights getting closer. A truck's horn. **BUG** *looks in its direction.* **BUG** *snuffs out their cigarette then throws themself in the path of the vehicle, landing with a smack.)*

(Inside the truck, **THIERRY** *is startled. Sitting next to him is* **BRUCE**, *unphased. Classic country music plays.[1])*

THIERRY. Another one!

BRUCE. Where?

THIERRY. Right there! He was HUGE. Left a smear.

BRUCE. Goddamn it.

THIERRY. Painted the windshield practically. That's maybe fifty in the past hour.

BRUCE. You been counting 'em?

THIERRY. Doesn't seem safe to drive with those guts all over the thing; obscures your vision.

BRUCE. Don't get your painties bunched up. I'll try the wipers.

---

1. A license to produce *BUGS* does not include a performance license for any third-party or copyrighted music. Licensees should create an original composition or use music in the public domain. For further information, please see the Music and Third-Party Materials Use Note on page iii.

*(**BRUCE** turns on the wipers. **BUG**, still dead on the front of the truck, is wiped back and forth, but not off.)*

THIERRY. You're making it worse. Let's just pull over.

BRUCE. What? Why?

THIERRY. We clean her up, start fresh. It'll take just a second.

BRUCE. No way.

THIERRY. Real quick?

BRUCE. Why're you riding my ass about this, Thierry? We got deadlines.

THIERRY. We always got deadlines.

BRUCE. We make it through Iowa by ten, we get a bonus.

THIERRY. Just wanna be safe, that's all.

BRUCE. You want that bonus, don't ya?

THIERRY. Yeah. *(A beat.)* How many bonuses you got?

BRUCE. Good amount lately.

THIERRY. Workin' overtime?

BRUCE. And nights. Gotta bring home the bacon.

THIERRY. Course, course. Think I could get on some of those?

BRUCE. You don't want those gigs. Trust me. They ain't for you.

*(**ANOTHER BUG** throws itself into the windshield. **THIERRY** stifles a scream.)*

Jesus Thierry!

THIERRY. Bruce let's pull over, can't we? Please?

BRUCE. What's got you all wound up, man?

THIERRY. Wanna clean up the windshield, is that so bad? It's like a...A murder scene out there.

BRUCE. Lay off it.

THIERRY. I mean – I mean, what if it's on purpose? If these bugs are killing themselves like on purpose?

BRUCE. God dammit.

THIERRY. Hear me out! Hear me out. In the past hour, we've hit fifty-four – And I have been counting – Fifty-four bugs along I-80. Now this rig here's about nine feet wide. Nine feet out of the whole entire, endless horizon, these bugs are landing within a nine foot goal post. That's like – That's needle in a haystack odds, not even taking into account how tiny the things are!

BRUCE. Come on now...

THIERRY. Doesn't it seem like there's something to that?! It's like these critters are trying to make themselves go SPLAT!

BRUCE. Don't be stupid. It's simple math. There've gotta be, what? A billion bugs here in Iowa; flying all around, all the time. It's – It's fish in a barrel is what it is.

THIERRY. Just can't stand the idea that they're offing themselves on our cab; like we're responsible.

BRUCE. Responsible? The hell do you mean "responsible"?

THIERRY. Like we're an accessory! We're an accessory Bruce, we gotta pull over!

BRUCE. Would you get a hold of yourself!

THIERRY. We have become death, destroyer of worlds! For whatever reason all these sweet little fellas are committing suicide right here on our watch!

BRUCE. So what? Is that some big emergency? If these flies wanna go and end it all, shouldn't that be their prerogative?

THIERRY. Prerogative?

BRUCE. I mean their right.

THIERRY. I know what prerogative means, I'm tryna wrap my head round how you could say that.

BRUCE. Say what? What am I saying?

THIERRY. Like it's okay to – to kill yourself!

BRUCE. Who says it ain't? I sure don't.

THIERRY. You know what / you sound like? You sound like a real class-A asshole! Capital A, capital S, Capital S, Capital –

BRUCE. I mean life is generally pretty shitty, right? Who am I to judge? If bugs or people or whatever wanna kill themselves, I say go ahead!

THIERRY. BRUCE!

> (A **THIRD BUG** *sends itself careening into the windshield.* **THIERRY** *recoils like he's trying to escape.*)

PULL OVER! You pull over right now –

BRUCE. Ain't no way / I'm gonna –

THIERRY. Else I swear to god I'm gonna piss all over this cab!

BRUCE. The FUCK?!

THIERRY. I am loaded with Arizona and Mountain Dew, brother. I'll soak this thing like a hose!

BRUCE. You've lost it! / Completely lost it!

THIERRY. Don't think I won't do it! Just you watch!

> (**THIERRY** *unzips his pants and whips out his –.*)

BRUCE. *(Swerving.)* JESUS MARY AND JOSEPH!

> (**BRUCE** *veers the truck to the side of the road and stops the engine. The music stops.* **THIERRY** *scampers outside, hyperventilating.* **BRUCE** *follows.)*

You got a good five seconds to explain yourself before I leave you out here in the –

THIERRY. Shovel. Where's the shovel?

BRUCE. Back of the cab. Christ almighty...

> (**THIERRY** *goes to the back of the truck. He returns with a shovel and furiously starts digging.)*

I can't understand it, I really can't. You bet your ass I'm calling HR about this.

THIERRY. We're gonna bury them. We're gonna bury those poor little critters. We're gonna give them a nice service and you're gonna help me. And you're / not gonna make fun of me. And you're gonna open up your heart and mourn for them and you're gonna ACTUALLY FEEL SOMETHING FOR ONCE IN YOUR GODDAMN LIFE!

BRUCE. I swear to god, man, swear to god I don't know what has happened to you. You fell off the deep end! Used to do these long hauls like it was nothing, we could –

> (**BRUCE** *is silenced by* **THIERRY**'s *sudden outburst.)*

I feel things.

THIERRY. No you don't.

BRUCE. Sure do. I feel like an idiot sitting here on the side of the road.

THIERRY. You know how many miles you and I put in together?

BRUCE. How many?

THIERRY. Twenty-four thousand, six hundred and eighty-one. And a half. In all that time, how much have we ever talked about ourselves?

BRUCE. You won't shut up about yourself. I know you better than your proctologist.

THIERRY. Well I know nothing, Bruce! I don't know a damn thing; it was a big day when I learned your wife's name. Nothing!

BRUCE. What does this have to do with all these –

THIERRY. I don't know. I really don't. Alls I know is I've got fifty-five dead bugs here and I can't help but feel like they knew what they were doing when they flew into that windshield and you don't seem to care and that terrifies me cuz I just think about all the times we're driving and you just keep staring and staring out the window and it's like there's something there. Something you don't let anybody get to, not even yourself, and when –

BRUCE. Thierry, woah. Listen to yourself.

THIERRY. *(Tearing up/crying.)* And when I hear you say "Well why shouldn't they kill themselves?" I wonder what's going on, but you never tell me nothing! And I – God – I'm starting to worry you might try to kill yourself too like the bugs or like my sister or –

BRUCE. Sister? Hold up, what happened to your sister?

THIERRY. She tried to fucking kill herself, man!

BRUCE. Jeeeeeezus, dude. When was this?

THIERRY. Few weeks ago. Really balled it up too. Ate a bunch of fiberglass insulation so she'd look all normal for the funeral. Thought it'd tear up her insides, but it just plugged her up and she had to have some of her intestine removed and now she's gotta poop into a lil' bag!

BRUCE. Thierry! Look at me. Look. I am fine, okay? I'm not gonna kill myself or eat a bunch of fiberglass like Barbara –

THIERRY. Dianne.

BRUCE. Dianne. Shit. Point is I am fine, alright? I'm A-Okay. Sure I don't...Don't put it all out there the way you do. So what? I'm not like you. I don't need to go on and on about my plantar warts or whatever to feel good about myself.

THIERRY. Yeah...Yeah, no, you're right.

BRUCE. You bet I am. How are those warts, by the way?

THIERRY. They're better, thanks.

BRUCE. You gonna be okay?

THIERRY. I am. Sorry if I'm being all – all invasive and shit.

BRUCE. Had me worried you'd gone soft. Now you still gotta pee, or was that just a bluff?

THIERRY. Naw I actually gotta go real bad. Will you at least scrape off the rest of those bugs?

BRUCE. Course, buddy.

> (He takes a wiper out of the cab as **THIERRY** scampers O/S. **BRUCE** watches him go, shaking his head. When he wipes the windshield, one by one the **BUGS** come loose.)

God damn Thierry. God damn.

> (A truck horn. **BRUCE** stops what he's doing and looks in that direction. Headlights in the distance. **BRUCE** gazes into them, his face cold and empty. He steps into the road,

now illuminated by the headlights growing brighter and brighter. Frantic honking is heard. **BRUCE** *starts to breathe heavily, his eyes pinched shut, fists clenched. At the last possible second,* **BRUCE** *jumps out of the path of the headlights. The sound of the passing rig fades. Crickets, owls in the distance. Country stillness.)*

*(***BRUCE***'s breathing has yet to subside. He takes the squeegee, and continues to wipe the windshield. He finishes and tries to shake the bug viscera loose. It won't come off. He begins to sob, and uses his hands to wipe the blade clean. It comes off in globs and sticks to him. Frantically he rubs his hands on his chest, his pants, then in the dirt at his feet. He collapses against the cab, crying. The moment hangs, then* **THIERRY** *returns.)*

THIERRY. I have never pissed so long in my – Bruce? What's the – Aw man, what's wrong?

BRUCE. Nothing! Nothing, I – *(He takes a deep breath, starting to compose himself.)* Those poor little bugs. It's...It's a damn shame.

THIERRY. Ain't it just. Hey there. Hey, it's good, buddy. You and I, we're alright. Alright now.

*(***THIERRY*** *helps* **BRUCE** *to his feet.)*

BRUCE. So do we...What? Say grace?

THIERRY. I think we gotta say a Hail Mary or something?

BRUCE. You know the Hail Mary?

THIERRY. No.

BRUCE. Me neither.

(They stand there in a strange, contemplative silence.)

Well...

THIERRY. Yeah.

> (**THIERRY** *picks up the shovel.* **BRUCE** *kicks the dirt at his feet onto the shallow grave.*)

BRUCE. Better keep on then.

THIERRY. For sure.

> (*The two get back into the truck, the engine revs to life, music starts back up again[1], and they make their way back on to the road. Lights fade out on the pile of* **BUGS**.)

---

1. A license to produce *Bugs* does not include a performance license for any third-party or copyrighted music. Licensees should create an original composition or use music in the public domain. For further information, please see the Music and Third-Party Materials Use Note on page iii.

If All That You Take From This Is Courage, Then I've No Regrets

Nicholas Pilapil

IF ALL THAT YOU TAKE FROM THIS IS COURAGE, THEN I'VE NO REGRETS was originally produced at the 47th Annual Samuel French Off Off Broadway Short Play Festival in August 2022. The performance was directed by directed by Nicholas Polonio. The cast was as follows:

LYDIA. . . . . .Lydia Gaston
ALEX . . . . Ethan Tampus
GISELLE . . . . .Joyce Lao

IF ALL THAT YOU TAKE FROM THIS IS COURAGE, THEN I'VE NO REGRETS was commissioned by IAMA Theatre Company for Pass the Mic: A Play Festival Amplifying AAPI Voices in 2021. The performance was directed by Rodney To. The cast was as follows:

LYDIA. . . . . .Lydia Gaston
ALEX . . . . .Alexander Fox
GISELLE . . . . Giselle Tongi

CHARACTERS

LYDIA – Female, 60+, Filipina

Strong willed and feisty

Not a stereotypical frail old lady kind of grandmother

Fluent in English despite her Filipino accent

ALEX – Male, twenties to thirties, Filipino American

Lydia's grandson, Giselle's son

Whether or not it's true, he's one of those people that says "my grandma is my best friend."

GISELLE – Female, forties to fifties, Filipina American

Alex's mom, Lydia's daughter,

Also plays **NEWS REPORTER**

SETTING

A kitchen in a Filipino American household.

TIME

Summer of 2021.

AUTHOR'S NOTES

Italicized words are in *Tagalog*.
Translations shouldn't be provided for the audience.
The intention of words should be enough for audiences to understand.

Don't fall into the trap of making Lydia and Alex too sentimental. Lydia and Alex should have a high stakes back and forth.
Take each (beat) deliberately.

A slash (/) means the character with the next line of dialogue begins their speech An em-dash (—) means a lingering thought not verbalized or a connecting thought.

(The sound of a staccato thud begins offstage, in the distance – it gets steadily closer.)

(Somewhere in the dark, a small TV screen flickers on with a screen of static veiled over a news channel.)

NEWS REPORTER. *(Voice-over.)* From brutal assaults on Asian senior citizens in the Bay Area to the deadly shootings of six Asian women at Atlanta-area spas, hate crimes against Asians rise in an epidemic of hate.

(The screen blacks out.)

(Lights up on a kitchen: on the wall a photo of the last supper, an old gas stove with a cast iron, on the counter Datu Puti soy sauce and vinegar, a rice cooker, and a small TV. The kitchen looks stuck in the past – but it's cozy.)

*(**LYDIA** stands at a counter, butchering a whole chicken on a wooden cutting board. The butchering sounds match the rhythm of the mysterious thud.)*

(The sound starts to fade as the lights get brighter and stops when –.)

*(**ALEX** rushes in.)*

ALEX. Mama, what are you doing?!

LYDIA. I'm making your favorite.

ALEX. You're supposed to be resting.

LYDIA. *Susmaryosep.*[1] *Lumayas ka nga.*[2]

ALEX. You literally just got jumped by some Steve Buscemi-looking motherfucker. Let me / do that for you.

> (**ALEX** *tries to take the knife out of* **LYDIA***'s hand. But she holds tight and slaps* **ALEX***'s hand away.*)

LYDIA. Ay. *Tang ina mo.*[3]

ALEX. You're still hurt.

LYDIA. Worse things are giving me pain.

Like you in my ass.

> (*He tries to take the knife from her again.*)

Walang hiya ka![4]

ALEX. Would you just let me help.

LYDIA. Make the rice.

ALEX. You make rice!

> (*Threateningly yet jokingly, she pulls the knife on him.*)

LYDIA. Do the garlic, then.

> (**ALEX** *takes the knife and works on the garlic. Smashing each clove before cutting it.*)

> (**LYDIA** *disappears and we hear something like rain falling – it's the sound of rice being poured into a pot. She reappears holding that pot of rice.*)

I should've *palo*'d[5] you more.

---

1. a contraction of Jesus, Mary, and Joseph
2. Get away from me.
3. Motherfucker.
4. You have no shame!
5. spanked

ALEX. If you remember correctly, that crack in your wooden spoon, over there, is from child abuse. My child abuse.

LYDIA. Cause you're *tigas ang ulo*.[1] You never listen to me.

ALEX. *(Playfully.)* You're such a bitch.

LYDIA. What was it again. The one you said before to your *tito*[2] Boy?

ALEX. "My grandma is a bad bitch!"

LYDIA. Yes that's the one.

I like that that one.

Resilient, strong.

I'm a "bad bitch."

ALEX. You know —

You don't have to be so strong all the time.

LYDIA. *Ang aking puke*[3] created three generations / here

ALEX. Please stop talking about your "pussy."

LYDIA. Your grandma is the strongest person you will ever know.

> (**LYDIA** *playfully smacks* **ALEX** *on the behind with the wooden spoon.*)

ALEX. Why is everyone even coming over?

LYDIA. We're family. It's what we do.

ALEX. Like really they couldn't skip one family Saturday for like once ever?

I don't know, so maybe, you can recuperate from a literal hate crime?

---

1. stubborn; hardheaded
2. uncle
3. my pussy

LYDIA. Without family, Alex, all we have is prayer.

ALEX. You should be high off a perc or drugged out on Ambien right now.

>   (**ALEX** *starts to move on with the recipe like it's second nature.*)

LYDIA. Did I teach you how to make that?

ALEX. I may not be Filipino enough to understand this co-dependency that makes you people flock together like sky rats every weekend. But I'm Filipino enough to know how to cook chicken adobo.

LYDIA. You're very messy, *Apo[1]*.

>   (**LYDIA** *cleans around him.*)

ALEX. You realize that all you people do is eat and stay on Facebook at these things anyways, right?

LYDIA. You just can't understand us.

We also *tsismis[2]* about you and your cousins and your *ninang's[3]* new nose.

ALEX. Your fault. You never taught us.

LYDIA. What. You wanted to sound like a FOB?

ALEX. It just would've been nice to...I don't know, understand, or be...or actually feel Filipino around all you old people.

LYDIA. *Matanda na[4]* — old? I still look good for my age, *ha[5]*.

Your other *lola[6]* isn't skinny like this.

---

1. Grandson
2. gossip
3. godmother's
4. old
5. an interjection; similar to "huh"
6. grandmother

ALEX. Yeah, well, Dad's mom is dead, so —

LYDIA. And you're not Filipino?

Look, you're cooking Filipino food right now, are you not?

ALEX. You know what I meant.

LYDIA. We gave you a gift.

We let you be American.

ALEX. Is that really a gift?

LYDIA. We gave you a country that was yours and would always have enough for you. You know in the Philippines, in school, we learn American history too. They taught us politics, and to speak English. Did you know that? They wanted to give us American values. They were selling to us hope. Just like your crazy *tita¹*, who is always scheming, and selling that Avon.

ALEX. I didn't know all that.

LYDIA. You shouldn't have to —

You're American.

You date white people.

You. You were born with hope — and you got it for free.

ALEX. Okay but like you too! You're pretty fucking American to me. Like, you aren't walking down the street in a success perm that screams Top Ramen Oriental flavoring. To the eye you look just like those dolled up real estate agents on those free notepads we get spammed. You look like you belong here.

> (**LYDIA** *turns on the sink and starts the long process of washing rice. We hear sounds of water running and the steady swish-swish of rice swirling in the pot.*)

---

1. aunt

LYDIA. *Apo*, look. Pretend we are the rice. Filipinos. The Koreans. Vietnamese. Chinese people. And America is the pot. We put in the rice to cook it. Right? Cause when the rice is cooked, it's at its full potential. *Pero[1]* you have wash it first. And that's the real part of making *kanin[2]*. It's not cooking, it's the washing. But when you wash the rice: pour the water, mix your fingers, swish it, disturb it, the water gets cloudy. Almost like the rice is losing its color.

> *(She pours out cloudy white water from the pot, and refills it again – swish-swish.)*

That's us. When we come here we have to wash ourselves of our past. We swish and swish and we let our color bleed out to become part of this country — to be our full potential. *Pero.* When you wash the rice, no matter how many times, even when the water is clear. The rice stays white. It's the same. We work hard to scrub ourselves of everything we've ever known because they tell us we have to, but it doesn't matter. Cause why? They will still see our color. No matter how many American values we have or how much American spirit lives in us — that's all they see of us.

May sasabihin ako sayo[3] the government they recruited people like us! Did you know that? They kept all the other Asians out for the longest time but you know what? They still let us in. Filipinos. They promised us more than what we had. So we came, we worked, worked for them, sacrificed for their people and their land, but even after all of that too, they don't accept us. We will always be different.

That's why I didn't teach your mommy to speak *Tagalog*.

---

1. but
2. cooked rice
3. I have to tell you something

So she wouldn't teach you. So nothing could hold you back.

You know why? Cause so much was already going to.

> (**LYDIA** *finishes washing the rice and brings the pot to the rice cooker.*)

Maybe that was my mistake.

ALEX. Why didn't you ever tell us this stuff growing up?

LYDIA. I taught you to cook rice.

ALEX. Why not your literal text book analogies of racism? No one ever tells us about that shit as kids. We had to learn it all on our own. Was it like wishful thinking that I would never have to deal with it?

LYDIA. I don't like being defined by my pain.

ALEX. Totally / but —

LYDIA. I never wanted to be known for what hurt us.

ALEX. But you and Papa immigrated here to give us a better life. I get it, like, yeah, trauma and stuff, but having those lessons growing up. I mean, I don't know, but don't you think it would've have made things easier for us?

LYDIA. I didn't come here for you.

ALEX. What?

LYDIA. *Oo.*[1] Everyone thinks immigrants, we flee our home to come here. Why? For a better life for our kids. But I didn't. I did it for myself first.

ALEX. Oh.

---

1. Yes.

LYDIA. You and your cousins look at us, your *lolas*, Papa, and me, like wantless, sexless, helpless. But, *hindi*[1]. I'm not helpless, Alex.

ALEX. I know you're not helpless.

But, like, I can't help wanting to help you.

I mean, I'm a nurse.

It's actually my job to help.

LYDIA. Okay, *ha*, but don't let me hold you back, *Apo*.

ALEX. You're my grandma. You may have not come here for me, so you say, but you still went through a lot, so that somehow, I ended up where I am today.

LYDIA. I was never trying to keep secrets.

I only never wanted you to feel bad about going after what you want.

And I never wanted you or your mommy to feel like the world was going to stop you from trying.

ALEX. I get that.

LYDIA. And you know what?

ALEX. What?

LYDIA. You're fearless because of it.

> (*Some kind of shift – maybe in time or memory. Maybe it's something only* **LYDIA** *can see or feel. Perhaps it plays off just like it's a typical beat.*)

And I was so proud of you.

I was proud to be your grandma.

ALEX. What do you mean was? I'm here right now, crazy lady.

Cooking for all those people coming over.

1. no

LYDIA. *Oo*. You're here, because I need you to be.

ALEX. That's why I'm your favorite grandchild.

> *(Beat.)*

LYDIA. Do you know why, even when it seems like I can't, why I still cook for my family?

ALEX. Generational trauma.

LYDIA. Because, I've been lucky to have so much more in life.

It's my duty.

ALEX. You're the best of us, Mama.

We all know it, even if we never tell you.

> *(Beat.)*

LYDIA. But why then if I sacrifice so much does God take so much away from me?

> *(Beat.)*

Why didn't you stop going to work during COVID?

ALEX. Was that an option?

LYDIA. It wasn't safe.

ALEX. It's an honor to be in a position to help.

That's what you've always taught us, right?

LYDIA. It was me —

ALEX. Of course it was you. Like you just said. It's duty.

I'm young and healthy, I do yoga. I'm literally the best candidate to be on the front line.

ALEX. So, if I don't do the job, then like, aren't I just running away from my responsibility.

LYDIA. Not many people are blessed enough to be some one who can bless others.

ALEX. I guess we really are lucky then.

LYDIA. *Salamat¹.*

ALEX. For what?

LYDIA. Taking care of me.

Even now.

> (*The sound of the thud returns softly, in the distance – steadily getting closer.*)

ALEX. I'm always going to be here take care of you.

LYDIA. Forever a nurse, *ha*?

> (**GISELLE** *enters – dressed in all black – and the sound stops.*)

GISELLE. Mommy, who are you talking to?

LYDIA. Nobody. Just cooking.

GISELLE. Why? I told you the reception is catered.

> (*Beat.*)

That was his favorite.

LYDIA. You should be resting.

> (*Beat.*)

GISELLE. Please leave it. Go get ready for the service.

> (*They walk offstage.* **ALEX** *continues cooking on his own.*)

---

1 Thank you.

(The sound of the thud softly fades back in as the lights fade to black. Then the TV flickers back on.)

NEWS REPORTER. *(Voice-over.)* COVID-19 is taking a devastating toll on Filipino American nurses. Even though Filipino nurses make up just four percent of the nursing population nationwide, nearly a third of the nurses who've died of coronavirus in the US are Filipino.

(The TV blacks out, and the sound of the thud continues in the dark. Then the sound slowly fades away like a sigh of relief.)

Shark Week

Erika Phoebus

SHARK WEEK was first produced by the Theatre 4the People in the 47th Annual Off Off Broadway Short Play Festival, in August 2022. The performance was directed by Katelynn Kenney. The Stage Manager was Jasia Ries. The cast was as follows:

KYRI... Aubrey Clyburn

ALEX .... Evan Frazier

DREW ....John Dimino

SHARK... Matt Giroveanu

CHARACTERS

KYRI – Seventeen, a lifeguard, a straight-A student. (*she/her*)

ALEX – Seventeen, a lifeguard, she's a fast talker and an even faster thinker. (*she/her*)

DREW – Seventeen, a lifeguard, scared, but he's really trying. (*he/him*)

SHARK – An apparition, a wondrous queer miracle, but also, really a shark. In drag. (*Any and all pronouns may apply.*)

SETTING

A beach.
Under the ocean.
Inside Kyri's head.

TIME

Summer.
The recent past.
A time when cell phones exist.

(A hot summer day. The ocean is post-storm pretty...untamed.)

*(**ALEX** sits in a tall lifeguard chair. **KYRI** stands in the sand next to her.)*

ALEX. Okay, then I can't go in the water today.

KYRI. You can still go in the water.

ALEX. No. I only have one tampon and it's inside me. If I go into the water, it's gonna fill up too fast. Then what? I free bleed into the ocean for the rest of our shift? Gross.

KYRI. That's not how tampons work.

ALEX. And this chair is white. I could stain it if I leak. I canNOT have that coming out of my paycheck. Plus, my mom would kill me.

KYRI. Yea but like...she'd get over it eventually... / right?

ALEX. No. Double plus, sharks are bad this year. Sharks love periods, obviously, so...

KYRI. Sharks are bad every year

ALEX. Exactly. Sharks are so fucked up. They're mean as shit. And we can't save lives if we get eaten. So let's stay alive. And pray my tampon's as super as the box says.

(Cracks herself up.)

*(**KYRI** stares out at the ocean.)*

Hey. Did you hear what I said? I said – You okay? I promise I'm not mad. I mean, sure, it _was_ your turn to bring back up tamps, like, I _was_ relying on that, but it's fine, we'll figure it –

(Blows her whistle. Again. Again.)

ALEX. AWAY FROM THE JETTIES! SWIM AWAY
FROM THE – Jesus Christ.

KYRI. They can't hear you, waves are loud today... And if
the world wants a shark to eat you, I don't think there's
anything you can do about it.

ALEX. I could not go into the ocean. Which is my whole
point. Unless this asshole gets his brains bashed in by
the jetties, then I'm fucked.

(Blows her whistle.)

You sure you don't have an extra tampon?

KYRI. No, I already said.

ALEX. You never forget your turn. Never. Like...Who even
are you right now? You never forget anything ever.

KYRI. I know haha so dumbed. I'm so dumb. The dumbest.
Like...

ALEX. Seriously though, you're on your period too. We're
synced so...How'd you forget?

KYRI. I said sorry / alright?

ALEX. Kyri –

KYRI. So just stop / it.

ALEX. Kyri –

KYRI. I said stop.

    (Beat.)

ALEX. Drew told me to tell you he wants to talk. And I told
him his haircut looks bad and to stay away. I don't care
if we're working the same shift, I don't care if we have
to swim far the fuck out there and save someone's life
and like be a team, or whatever, I don't care. Because
fuck him. So...yea. Just wanted you to know.

(Beat.) And fuck him for hurting you, like, fuck him for not being everything you ever dreamed he'd be.

KYRI. No I'm fine, so fine. Honestly? It's a mature hurt, breaking up, so that's cool, um, can we go back to the, the period thing because I need to, to talk to you, I need to talk to you about...

ALEX. ...Oh. My. God. Oh my god KYRI! How could you not tell me!?!

KYRI. I know, I'm sorry, I just, I didn't know how to –

ALEX. Areyouwearingoneofthoseohmygodwhataretheycalled uhhh...DivaCups!? And you didn't tell me!? What does it feel like going in...did you like it? Stop! Ohmygod or like period panties? Can you wear those with a swim suit, no right? So what are you doing, like, for real ohmygod are you free bleeding!? Tell me everything ohmygod I love you so much

KYRI. That guy's getting close to the jetties again.

> *(They both blow their whistles.)*

ALEX. I mean, who the hell swims after a storm. So selfish. Don't you think it's selfish?

> *(**KYRI** shrugs.)*

Would you go swimming after a storm? And risk getting sucked out to sea, or getting eaten by sharks, or getting your head bashed in by the jetties unless some beautiful lifeguards like us swam out into those treacherous waters to save you?

KYRI. But, wait, so like...if he gets hurt, you think it's like... punishment? Or something?

ALEX. I mean obviously we'd do our jobs and like...*try*...

ALEX. But it would definitely be his fault. Like that time Jeremy kept trying to shoot erasers out of his nose in bio cus he wanted Amber to see how strong his lung capacity was so she would make out with him? And we all told him like, ew stop, and then one of the erasers got stuck up his nose and he freaked out and sort of snorted the eraser, like, up?

And it got stuck somewhere between his nose and his brain And then his uncle had to like, stop his matinee or whatever, showed up at school, full drag, his uncle's a drag queen. Like, he's an actor, but he also does drag

KYRI. I know, she's like...really good.

ALEX. Right!? Like...that padding ohmygod, anyway, and now Jeremy's nose is all fucked from the surgery for doing stupid shit. So...yea, his fault. Same thing.

KYRI. Wait...what?

ALEX. Twizzler?

KYRI. No thanks...That was cool of his uncle to help him. Don't you think that was cool?

ALEX. I guess. *(Re: swimmer by the jetties.)* Stupid piece of –

(Whistle.)

I mean, here we are, putting our lives on the line. Every day. The ocean is no joke. And my ass isn't this muscle fat just to save some macho moron's –

(Whistle.)

Ohmygod crampsssss. The whistle hurts my – Shit.

> *(She deeply, dramatically inhales through her nose. One. Two. Three. Four.)*
>
> *(Holds for seven.)*
>
> *(She exhales a loud whooshing sound.)*
>
> *(One. Two. Three. Four. Five. Six. Seven. Eight.)*

My mom taught me this for my anxiety, but it helps with shark week too.

(Whistle. Whistle.)

Come on free bleeder, join me.

(Inhale two three four...)

KYRI. It's fine, I got it.

> *(**KYRI** walks towards the ocean.)*
>
> *(Blows her whistle.)*
>
> *(Hand signals to swim away from the jetties.)*
>
> *(She starts running.)*
>
> *(Whistle. Running. Hand signals.)*

ALEX. *(From **KYRI**'s mind.)* It would definitely be his fault.

> *(**KYRI** blows her whistle. Hand signals.)*

Like...who even are you right now.

> *(**KYRI** blows her whistle. Hand signals.)*

All because he was doing stupid shit. So...yea, his fault. Same thing.

> *(**KYRI** blows her whistle. Hand signals.)*

And fuck him for hurting you. Fuck him. Fuck him. Fuck him.

> *(Hand signals. Hand signals. Hand signals. It's becoming a sort of swimming motion.)*
>
> *(Big wave crash. Breath. Breath. It's kind of hard to breathe? The sound of another whistle. Something's not quite right...)*

(DREW dreamily runs over.)

DREW. Hey. Thanks. Didn't see that guy. Was trying to get that other guy to watch his kid. Waves are wild today.

KYRI. Yea. So wild.

DREW. Cus of the storm.

KYRI. Big storm.

DREW. So big.

KYRI. The biggest.

DREW. Right?

KYRI. Yea. *(Beat.)* I didn't come down here because you wanted me to. Just so you know. I left my station because someone was in trouble. And you didn't see that he was in trouble. Even though that's your job. You didn't really understand the trouble he was in.

DREW. Okay...Well tell me about it then, / help me –

KYRI. I shouldn't have to tell you about it, you should just –

DREW. – know. I should just know, you're right.

KYRI. Forget it, I'm going back – Wait what?

DREW. You're right. I should know. But I don't. Cus I'm dumb.

KYRI. Oh. Wow. I mean, yes.

DREW. This is my fault too.

KYRI. Oh, wow. Yea, yes, it –

DREW. Which is why I told my mom.

> *(KYRI tries to take a breath...but can't. Her body jolts, as if hit by a wave.)*

KYRI. ...You...what?

DREW. Look, I know you said don't tell / my mom –

KYRI. Your mom's going to tell / *my* mom –

DREW. And I promise, I heard / you but –

KYRI. Does my mom know? / Did your mom call or –

DREW. I don't know, what? No.

KYRI. Oh my god. Oh my god! She's going to kill me, my mom is going to kill me.

DREW. I mean, no maybe not.

KYRI. I HATE YOU!

DREW. It's gonna be okay –

KYRI. I should have never let you in. Like, in all the ways. Like, emotionally but also like...in the other way too. Especially the other way. I just – I fucking – It hurts. / So much.

DREW. I know. I know, I –

KYRI. You left this, this ache, inside my stomach, like my heart was in my stomach and turns out it's a a a a fucking...actual...*(Gasp.)* actual *(Gasp.)* ac –

(She's having trouble breathing.)

DREW. I'm scared too Kyri! I was scared and and I had to tell someone cus cus I didn't know what you'd do...what if you – and that secret? *(Suddenly haunted, distorted.)* It's sharp. It's hungry. And it would eat you alive, 'til there was nothing left but the stain on your soul, like... forever.

KYRI. Help.

DREW. And I couldn't do that to you or me or anyone, your parents, to fucking Alex, who I still don't like –

KYRI. Help.

DREW. She's still an asshole to me most of the time –

KYRI. Help.

DREW. But I couldn't bear thinking...What if you weren't okay, in an even bigger way than this, like what if you were eternally not okay and, and I had to –

KYRI. Somebody he –

> (*Whistle. Whistle. Whistle. Whistle. WhistleWhistleWhistleWhistle.*)

> (**ALEX** *runs past. Everything starts swirling.*)

ALEX. KYRI!

> (**DREW** *and* **ALEX** *disappear into the ocean.* **KYRI** *tries to breathe. Tries to breathe. Why can't she fucking –.*)

> (*Darkness...*)

> (*A* **SHARK** *appears.*)

KYRI. Are you going to eat me?

SHARK. No.

KYRI. Are you not going to eat me because I missed my period?

SHARK. Haha. No.

KYRI. But...I thought you liked that kind of thing. Sharks like blood, or, whatever.

SHARK. That's true. And periods are great. But not for eating. Actually that's not true, I don't like...fear menstruation. I'm not a monster.

KYRI. ...Ew.

SHARK. But humans don't taste all that great, period. Ha! Get it? Period?

> (**KYRI** *starts crying.*)

Oh, hey, hey, babe, don't worry...when I bite a human, I usually just throw it back. Catch and release. And I *definitely* don't come up here looking for a shedder. That time of the month hurts enough as it is, you know what I mean?

KYRI. Yea...Kind of...*(Cries harder, the flood gates open.)* No. I don't know what you're saying at all, I'm so sorry, I'm such a fuck up, I can't even understand a. Simple. Thing. A shark. Is saying!

(Sobbing.)

SHARK. Okay. Babe. Wow, breathe.

KYRI. I can't!

SHARK. That's fair. Okay. Listen. Are you listening?

KYRI. Yea I'm really trying to listen, I'm trying so hard.

SHARK. Okay, great. Because this is important. For both of us.

KYRI. Okay sorry, yea, sorry.

SHARK. This whole...sharks love periods, they're coming for us thing? It's old, it's insulting, and frankly, don't you humans do enough to pray on uteruses? But we're still saying the sharks are out to get you? Talk about ew.

KYRI. OHMYGOD YOU'RE SO RIGHT!! I am part of the problem, I'm sorry, I'm trash, I –

SHARK. Hey, hey, hi, hey, look at my teeth. Look at my teeth. Are you looking at them?

KYRI. Yea. Um...They're big. Not big but like, sharp. There's a lot.

SHARK. Yea. Wanna count them?

KYRI. Uh *(Sniffle.)* Okay *(Sniffle.)* One. Two. Three...

*(**KYRI** silently counts. Her sniffles fade.)*

SHARK. Wanna tell me what's going on?

KYRI. Uhh, ok, I guess. You sure? It's kind of a lot.

SHARK. There's eighty-seven thousand pounds of plastic in the ocean, we're dying everyday, I think I can handle it.

KYRI. It's just, I'm um, in high school, which you can probably tell, I mean, people say I look old but still just like, high school old?

SHARK. Sure. Mature.

KYRI. Yea. I'm mature and in high school and just found out I'm...pregnant? Which sounds so just like, like a bad TV drama, you know? And I'm tired. Like, I'm not supposed to be the bad guy, I get straight A's and my show choir just won state.

SHARK. Mmhmm. Been there.

KYRI. Ohmygod what voice part were you? Let me guess...

SHARK. Uh. No. But I do get a bad rap for being the big bad monster under the sea. I mean, have you seen *Jaws*? I, personally, have not. But that doesn't mean I'm not affected by the people who think I would ever become so obsessed with killing humans that I'd chase a boat around 'til I could finally tear it to shreds. What kind of shark in their right mind would *eat a boat*? Meanwhile, I'm over here trying to keep Shelly and her little chompy children moving along so they don't eat all the sea grass and destroy the balance of the entire ocean's ecosytem. I mean, if you wanna talk bad guys, let's talk about sea turtles. They are notorious for clapping back.

KYRI. I didn't know.

SHARK. No one ever does.

KYRI. Wow. That like...has nothing to do with what I'm going through. But thank you for sharing. If I survive, I promise to tell your story. People deserve to know.

SHARK. Thanks babe, but...Let me put it this way. Maybe I'm not so much a killer of life, but a protector of a different kind of life. Maybe I'm not a killer at all. MAYBE I'm just here to survive. And I do. Cus the ocean needs me, and I trust myself to know what to do to take care of it. Make sense?

KYRI. So...I should just...accept that I'm...pregnant, and learn how to take care of...it? A...baby...Cus that's how nature works?

SHARK. ...No. I mean...if that's what you want, go on and ride that wave. But what I'm really trying to say is...What if you didn't have to feel so bad about doing what's best for you and your ocean? For you and your spirit. Whatever that may be.

KYRI. You mean, like –

GROUP OF VOICES. *(Surrounding* **KYRI**.*)* WAVE!

DREW. Okay you're going to hold your breath in three, two –

　　(Crash. Big wave.)

　　*(***KYRI*** *and* ***DREW*** *go under.)*

GROUP OF VOICES. WAVE!

DREW. Hold your breath again in three, two –

　　(Crash. Big wave.)

　　Hold on to this. Keep holdng on.

KYRI. Help. Help. Help. / Help. Help. Help. Help. Help. Help. Help.

ALEX. WAVE!

DREW. We got you. Hold your breath in three, two –

KYRI. Drew?

ALEX. KYRI HOLD YOUR BREATH!

> *(Crash. Big wave. **KYRI**'s thrust onto shore.)*

KYRI. *(Gasp.)* I'm sorry *(Gasp.)* I'm sorry *(Gasp.)* I'm sorry *(Gasp.)* I'm sorry

> *(**DREW** wipes hair out of **KYRI**'s face. **ALEX** bats his hand away.)*

ALEX. Don't touch her. *(To **KYRI**.)* Hey babe, hey, it's me, hi. Can you hear me?

KYRI. *(Gasp.)* Yea.

ALEX. You okay?

KYRI. *(Gasp.)* Uh-huh

ALEX. You sure?

> *(**KYRI** nods.)*

Good. *(Beat.)* What the fuck is wrong with you, we never go out alone, not when the waves are like this, oh my god, we never. go out. alone. Kyri. We don't do that, we don't go out there without each other, I thought you fucking died trying to save that fucking asshole's life, by yourself, you could have died Kyri, what the fuck! *(To **DREW**.)* Can you make yourself useful and go like, fill out paperwork or something?

DREW. I, uh...It wasn't my fault, I swear, I was getting some dude to watch his kid, and then she came out of nowhere and got sucked into a riptide and, and that guy she went out for, he was fine, got himself out but, I mean, she knows better, swim parallel to the shore, she knows that's how to get out and she didn't, that's not / my fault

ALEX. Shut up. Just. Shut. Up!

KYRI. Don't tell my mom *(Gasp.)* don't tell my mom *(Gasp.)* don't tell my mom *(Big gasp.)* your fucking mom is going to tell my mom

ALEX. Our moms haven't talked since they chaperoned homecoming together like three years ago, what are you talking about? Cus of the punch bowl thing, did you hit your head?

DREW. I didn't tell my mom.

KYRI. Yes you did, you told me you did.

ALEX. Wait, his mom? What?

KYRI. You literally said "I told my mom" and then I told you I hated you and you said you were scared which I honestly felt kinda bad for you, but then –

DREW. I haven't talked to you since you told me you were – I mean I've been blowing up your phone trying to make sure YOU weren't gonna tell. Dude my mom would fucking kill me too. I have a basketball scholarship! Do you know what –

(**KYRI**'s *breathing picks up again.*)

ALEX. Go away Drew.

DREW. But –

ALEX. Don't you get it, she can't fucking breathe when you're around! Like, literally!

DREW. Jesus. Okay. I'm just trying to –

ALEX. GO!

(**DREW** *leaves.* **KYRI** *tries to catch her breath.*)

KYRI. *(Gasp.)* I – *(Gasp.)* I – *(Gasp.)* Shark *(Gasp.)* Where's my *(Gasp.)* Shark –

ALEX. Hey. Hey.

(**ALEX** *deeply inhales. One. Two –.*)

ALEX. Come on, do it with me.

> (*They inhale two three four. Hold seven.* **KYRI***'s body fights it. Exhale a loud whooshing sound.*)

Good. Again.

> (*Inhale. Hold. Loud whooshing sound. Inhale. Hold –.*)

KYRI. I'm pregnant...(*Beat.*) I'm sorry, it's fucked up I didn't tell you, you're my best friend and I didn't know how, I couldn't say it...That I was...I was...I mean I I I I I *am* –

> (**ALEX** *goes to speak.* **KYRI** *stops her.*)

> (*A quiet, sacred moment between very best friends. An understanding.*)

> (**ALEX** *gives* **KYRI** *space to speak.*)

> (**KYRI** *takes a deep breath.*)

I don't want it. Does that make me a bad person? Am I a bad person if I need it / gone –

> (**ALEX** *pulls* **KYRI** *into a hug, holding her tight.*)

Georgia Rose

Onyekachi Iwu

GEORGIA ROSE was originally developed for Two Strikes Theatre Collective's 2020 Brown Sugar Bake-Off. A staged reading of the play was presented at the 47th Annual Samuel French Off Off Broadway Short Play Festival on August 18th, 2022. The performance was directed by Onyekachi Iwu. Stage directions were read by Brianna Johnson. The cast was as follows:

CLAIRE JOHNSON .... Florence Taylor

AMY MORGAN .... Emory Kemph

CHARACTERS

CLAIRE JOHNSON – Early forties, Black, female, only wears lipstick to church, grocery shops in silk bonnets and family reunion T-shirts, never lost the baby weight.

AMY MORGAN – Early thirties, white, female, wears cherry lipstick to class, grocery shops in sports bras and pink yoga pants, lost her baby weight after four months.

SETTING

Warwick, Georgia.

TIME

April 2020.

AUTHOR'S NOTES

"/" indicates that the characters are speaking at the same time.

(SETTING: It is 5:50pm on a hot Thursday evening.)

(AT RISE: **MRS. AMY MORGAN** *sits in a Zoom call, perched against a plain white wall in her home. A bright sign hangs over her head that reads "Look And Listen".)*

(**MRS. MORGAN** *tightens her blonde ponytail. She turns up the corners of her clown-red mouth. She waits and waits awkwardly. Her face gradually slips into a glassy frown.)*

(A few moments later, **MS. CLAIRE JOHNSON***: enters the call. She sits in a tight, messy living room.* **MRS. MORGAN***'s smile quickly returns, like a restaurant flipping over the "OPEN" sign once again.)*

(**CLAIRE** *looks like she just walked out of a car crash. Her curly, "running-errands" wig sits on her head like a hat, clearly having been tossed on moments prior. She is in the middle of folding clothes. Her body is tired and hangs low, like a sidewalk couch.)*

(A dull scar lives on her right cheek.)

CLAIRE. Oh!

MRS. MORGAN. Hello, Ms. Johnson. How are you?

CLAIRE. I am so sorry. I wasn't expecting you to be all ready to go. I'm not late, am I?

MRS. MORGAN. No, actually we're –

CLAIRE. Hello? Hello?

MRS. MORGAN. Oh. Can you hear me, Ms. Johnson?

CLAIRE. Honey, I told you you can call me Claire!

MRS. MORGAN. Right. Claire. Sorry. My mother was a "yes sir" and "yes ma'am" kind of woman. Force of habit, I suppose.

>   (**CLAIRE** *moves the laundry basket from her lap to the floor. She keeps folding.*)

CLAIRE. Well, that's for children. We're not children, are we?

MRS. MORGAN. No.

CLAIRE. We're both adults. Can I call you Amy?

MRS. MORGAN. I prefer Mrs. Morgan.

CLAIRE. Alright. Well, I am so sorry, Mrs Morgan. I wasn't expecting you to be all ready to go. I'm not late, am I?

>   (**CLAIRE** *notices how crooked her wig is and tries to subtly adjust it.*)

MRS. MORGAN. Nope. We still got ourselves about five minutes 'til. But I'm ready to go if you are.

CLAIRE. I'm ready. I like to be early. I try to tell Destiny if you ain't early, you're fixing to be late.

MRS. MORGAN. Yes. Regarding Destiny –

CLAIRE. Plus, I ain't really adjusted to this whole video thing. I had to have my son Travis set it up for me. He's the computer wiz around here. I told him, he keep studying, he can be the next Mark Zuckerberg. You ever notice how Mark Zuckerberg don't look right?

MRS. MORGAN. Yes. Um. No. Anyway –

CLAIRE. Looks like a human that got turned inside out. You see that video of him in that courtroom? Up in there looking crazy! I tell Destiny you can always tell when somebody's lying if their eyes start looking crazy.

MRS. MORGAN. Yes. Well, anyway, about Destiny –

CLAIRE. How is your mother? She doing alright with everything? I remember back during orientation you said she wasn't doing too good.

MRS. MORGAN. She's fine. Well. She's dead.

CLAIRE. Oh. I'm so sorry.

MRS. MORGAN. But I'm fine. We weren't close. I actually would rather focus on Destiny. Is this a good time?

CLAIRE. *(To someone off-screen.)* QUIET I'M ON THE PHONE!

(To **MRS. MORGAN**.*)*

I'm so sorry. I told them I'd be on the phone. I'm so sorry about your mother.

MRS. MORGAN. You seem distracted. Is this a good time?

CLAIRE. *(To* **MRS. MORGAN**.*)* This is a perfect time. I usually work late, but I moved my hours around.

(To someone off-screen.)

Don't you see I'm on the phone? He's hungry. Go in there and fix him something.

(To **MRS. MORGAN**.*)*

Destiny's little brother just having a little cabin fever. Travis is taking care of it. Destiny's in there in the room sleep.

MRS. MORGAN. Oh, really? It's a bit early.

CLAIRE. She's always been like that. Sleeping at odd hours. You have a little one too, right? I remember you said you had a daughter.

MRS. MORGAN. Yes. She's been struggling a lot too with the transition. It's a very confusing time. Anyway, Ms. Johnson. The reason I wanted to speak with you was regarding Destiny's class performance.

CLAIRE. Right. Okay.

MRS. MORGAN. Today was the fifth time Destiny has refused to turn on her camera and participate in my class.

CLAIRE. Yes. I got your emails. Thank you for bringing this to my attention. I've been trying to tell her. She says she don't mean anything by it. She just gets overwhelmed. That's all.

MRS. MORGAN. I understand. Unfortunately, as I've told Destiny, I need all of my students to be visible to me. It communicates to me that they are listening and present. That's why I have this sign, see?

> (**MRS. MORGAN** *points to the sign above her head and smiles like she's in a yogurt commercial.*)

CLAIRE. She is listening. When I come back from work and ask how school was, she tells me exactly what y'all did. She just has trouble focusing when there's too much going on. She gets nervous.

MRS. MORGAN. Unfortunately, I can't make an exception for Destiny without making an exception for all of my students.

> (**CLAIRE** *mirrors* **MRS. MORGAN***'s plastic smile.*)

CLAIRE. I'll make sure she keeps it on next time. Is that all?

MRS. MORGAN. Unfortunately, no. She also hasn't been turning in her assignments.

CLAIRE. Right. She told me she was getting behind. She's a very honest child. I've been pulling extra hours at Winn-Dixie, so I told Travis to help her. He only just got back from college because they sent all the kids back home. So it was just me before. She'll do better.

MRS. MORGAN. What about her father?

CLAIRE. What about her father?

MRS. MORGAN. Well, I imagine if she had a father, that would lessen the burden on all of you.

CLAIRE. My daughter is not a burden.

MRS. MORGAN. Of course. I didn't mean –

CLAIRE. We're fine. She said she's working on catching up. Just give her time. You know, she even said she enjoys your class. You're one of her favorite teachers.

MRS. MORGAN. Ms. Johnson, your daughter called me a "stank-faced white bitch" in the middle of my class today.

> *(Pause.)*

Was she honest about that?

CLAIRE. She didn't mean that. She just gets frustrated sometimes and lashes out. I'll tell her to apologize.

MRS. MORGAN. That isn't the point.

CLAIRE. She knows that ain't appropriate. I'll talk to her. Actually, it looks like Travis may need some help. I appreciate your time, Mrs. Morgan. Is that all? Are we done?

MRS. MORGAN. Ms. Johnson, I'm afraid I will need to contact Destiny's case worker.

CLAIRE. What? Why?

MRS. MORGAN. Destiny was made very clear by the judge this semester /that her probation required that she complete her coursework.

CLAIRE. /Why would you do that? I don't think there's any need to do that. I'll talk to her.

MRS. MORGAN. I've tried talking to her, Ms. Johnson. I really do want her to succeed. But I can't help a young woman who doesn't want to help herself.

CLAIRE. So you're sending her to jail?

MRS. MORGAN. No. I just –

CLAIRE. You think that will make her better?

MRS. MORGAN. That isn't up to me. That will be up to the judge. This may surprise you, but I don't want this to happen any more than you do. I'm afraid I have no choice.

CLAIRE. You know this is wrong. You're sitting over there looking crazy. You know this ain't right. You're sending her to jail.

MRS. MORGAN. I am only notifying her caseworker.

CLAIRE. But you know what will happen.

MRS. MORGAN. She knew the consequences. I'm just not confident Destiny is committed to my classroom.

CLAIRE. What classroom? Y'all on a video! She was doing better before all this happened. It's not her fault. You even said your daughter was struggling right now too. If Destiny was a little white girl –

MRS. MORGAN. *(Shocked.)* Please. Ms. Johnson, this is not a race issue. I want us to stick to the facts here.

CLAIRE. Facts?

MRS. MORGAN. This simply comes down to behavior. Might I remind you, your daughter stabbed another student! And I believe –

CLAIRE. But that was months ago! What was she supposed to do?! Those little Black boys were following her around and putting their hands on her for weeks! We tried reporting it. Y'all didn't do nothing. Instead of punishing them, you punished her!

MRS. MORGAN. It is no singular incident, Ms. Johnson. She walked out of classrooms in the middle of lessons. She stole another student's wallet and lied about it. And she cursed out one of her teachers!

CLAIRE. But she's been doing better. She's just struggling with the video. She's a good girl.

MRS. MORGAN. That may be, but we can't deny the reason she is on probation is due to her hitting you.

(Pause.)

CLAIRE. You ain't never hit your mother before?

MRS. MORGAN. Excuse me?

CLAIRE. You said you weren't close. You never thought of hurting her? Getting back at her? Hit her like she could hit you?

(Pause.)

MRS. MORGAN. It's not what I thought of doing. It's what I chose to do.

CLAIRE. She's a good girl. She just lost control. I overreacted. I should have never called the police. I didn't know what else to do.

MRS. MORGAN. You knew exactly what to do. And you did the right thing. I'm just trying to do the right thing, Ms. Johnson. I'm trying to do what is best for her and for you. Destiny can be lovely when she chooses to be. But I can't keep making excuses for her. She intimidates the other students. She derails lessons and can be very mean. In fact, I have one Black male student whose home doesn't even have wifi right now. He does all of his lessons using his mother's phone hotspot. And he keeps his camera on. I'm not trying to be difficult. I have a duty to hold standards and report this behavior regardless of my personal feelings.

CLAIRE. This won't help her. All y'all do is judge her. What have you done for her?

MRS. MORGAN. I have offered Destiny multiple times to meet with me privately to go over the material, or to discuss her feelings, but she refused. Every time. I can't help a young woman who doesn't want to help herself.

CLAIRE. She's a girl.

MRS. MORGAN. What?

CLAIRE. She's not a woman. You keep calling her a woman. She's not grown. She's a girl. She's fourteen.

MRS. MORGAN. Ms. Johnson, we believe in holding students accountable here at Jefferson Academy. Perhaps this just isn't the right program for your daughter.

CLAIRE. I put her in this program because she's brilliant, and she earned her spot. Y'all just don't like Black girls.

MRS. MORGAN. Our school has a number of African American students who are excelling in our program.

CLAIRE. I didn't say African American. I said Black girls.

MRS. MORGAN. I don't understand –

CLAIRE. Y'all only like Black boys. Y'all like putting them on your little teams, or have them date your little white girls. They can be Sidney Poitier or Snoop Dogg. It don't matter. As long as they make y'all feel cool. But the Black girls are different. Y'all only like Black girls with white mamas. Or Black girls who try to look like white girls. Y'all can't stand Black girls like Destiny. She's too big and too Black for y'all. She look too much like her mama. Did you know one of those little Black boys said she looked like a man? If you had to listen to what those Black boys said to her, you'd stab a motherfucker too.

MRS. MORGAN. I'm very sorry Destiny was teased. I think she's a beautiful girl.

CLAIRE. She's not mean. She's just sad.

MRS. MORGAN. I understand.

CLAIRE. We're all a little sad right now. Doesn't she have a right to be sad?

MRS. MORGAN. I hear you, Claire.

CLAIRE. Do you?

MRS. MORGAN. I do. Sometimes the people we love give us bad days. My mother still gives me bad days. A lot of them, actually.

CLAIRE. And you still loved her, didn't you?

(**MRS. MORGAN** *isn't sure.*)

MRS. MORGAN. Of course. But regardless of my personal feelings, I have a duty to –

CLAIRE. *(To Travis.)* Take him outside! I don't care, Travis. Just take him outside. NOW!

(**CLAIRE**'s *eyes follow Travis until she's sure she's alone. She takes a breath and closes her eyes.* **MRS. MORGAN** *waits.*)

MRS. MORGAN. Claire? Are you alright?

CLAIRE. I know you got a duty. But it ain't her fault. I was sad when I was pregnant with Destiny. It's like smoking cigarettes or drinking. You ain't supposed to be sad when you're pregnant with a child, or you'll mess it up. I knew better than to be sad, but I just felt so alone. Everywhere I went, I felt a hole shaking in my chest.

CLAIRE. Night before I gave birth to Destiny, I was laid up in the tub. I fell asleep. And I remember sinking down and wanting to be dead. Feeling like no one would ever want me again. But in the dream, I saw her in my arms.

I was in a big field, butter sunshine coming down. I saw my mother and her mother wrapped around me like an envelope. And that's when I knew I would be alright. When she was born, the room felt like brown sugar and honey. Her skin felt like rose petals. I named her Destiny because God chose her for me.

MRS. MORGAN. I'm sorry.

CLAIRE. She's mean. She's violent. But she's also the one who reminds us to say grace. She packs my lunch in the morning. She watches golf, and she don't get bored. She's smart. She counts my change for me at the store. And she's funny. Did you know she loves Tony Bennett? Around Christmas time she likes to pretend to be Tony Bennett while I'm in the kitchen cooking. She sways her hips around with a wooden spoon and sings "Blue Velvet". She's sensitive. She's so many things. She's violent because she knows she deserves more. And nobody can give it to her. Not even me. She'll do better. I promise you that. Please.

(Silence.)

MRS. MORGAN. That scar on your face. That was her, right?

(Silence.)

The caseworker should be in touch with you tomorrow. Goodnight, Claire. I appreciate your time. Take care.

> (**MRS. MORGAN** *exits the Zoom call.* **CLAIRE** *is alone. The hole in her chest she's known since she was a little girl chews her up and sucks the air around her through a straw until she can't breathe.* **CLAIRE***'s eyes look off camera. She sees Destiny.)*

CLAIRE. Didn't I tell you to stay in your room and stay out of grown folks business? Aht! I don't want to hear it. Go put some shoes on and pack a bag. Don't worry about why. We're going for a drive. DO WHAT I TELL YOU! Always want to ask questions about every goddamn thing... I'm sorry, babygirl. For once, just do what I tell you. Alright?

(**CLAIRE** *closes her laptop and exits in a hurry.*)

End of Play

Too Much Lesbian Drama: One Star

Jessie Field

TOO MUCH LESBIAN DRAMA: ONE STAR was first produced by the 47th Annual Off Off Broadway Short Play Festival in August 2022. The performance was directed by Michele O'Brien. The Stage Manager was James Martinez Salem. The cast was as follows:

ADDISON .... Heather Sawyer

CARTER... River Stone

DOC/OTHERS................................... Danielle Koenig

CHARACTERS

ADDISON – is twenty-four. She is a young lesbian with young lesbian problems.

CARTER – is thirty-eight. She is really trying. The plants came with the office.

DOC, OTHERS – is fifty-five. Only high-level therapists give therapy to therapists, she likes to think.

Other characters that may or may not exist are surprises. Don't worry about it.

TIME

Last Tuesday. Then three Tuesday's from now. Then the Tuesday after that.

AUTHOR'S NOTES

CARTER's monologues are steady. **ADDISON**'s pick up speed and intensity like that boulder rolling after Indiana Jones, but she's never angry. The truth just tumbles out at a certain velocity.

(AT RISE: A nice office. Clinical, but warm. Books and plants. **ADDISON** *sits on a blue square couch.* **CARTER**, *on a matching blue armchair.)*

ADDISON. Soooo...

CARTER. Yes?

ADDISON. You're...fine? Doing well...I mean?

CARTER. Yes. As always.

ADDISON. Right.

CARTER. Addison...

ADDISON. It must be nice! I mean, always doing well.

CARTER. Once again –

ADDISON. I just truly admire that!

CARTER. Once again – this is your therapy session, and we've got less than five minutes left. Is there anything about *yourself* that you would like to talk about?

ADDISON. Oh no. I did the thing again.

CARTER. You did the thing again.

ADDISON. What does it mean, doc?

CARTER. It seems like it might be difficult for you to face yourself and what you're feeling.

ADDISON. Well! That's easy to say, isn't it? You sit there, observing me, and then I ask you to tell me the observations, and-and – you do!

CARTER. ...Yes.

ADDISON. Yes! And...you know what? It makes you a very good therapist. Incidentally, when did you decide to become a therapist and why?

CARTER. Addison.

ADDISON. *(This monologue starts extremely light-hearted and descends into madness.)* Oh, what do you want me to say? My name is *Addison*. I'm twenty-*four*. Sometimes I walk a full mile out of my way to work so that I won't pass any buildings with reflective windows because starting my day with my grotesque reflection in my mind ruins it...And then tada! I'm the girl who cries at work and everybody notices EXCEPT for the woman I've been in love with for two years who is busy flirting with some piece of shit named CHARLIE, even though there's nothing remarkable about him AT ALL. And SHE is *so. Remarkable,* doc. But she won't talk to ME anymore because I told her I loved her last Tuesday –

CARTER. *(Internally: !!!)* What?

ADDISON. – YEAH, and it turns out she's not bisexual, actually, she just likes the IDEA of being bi and was trying it out by flirting with me – like she admitted she was flirting with me! But then she said that we shouldn't talk anymore which is completely fine except it feels like dying and now when I walk past those reflective buildings I see her instead of me and I have to wonder if this happened – if she rejected me – because I'm too fat or too gay or just because I'm too MUCH. Like you get past the quiet considerate part of myself and there's just this FLOOD and people can't handle it, ya know? Or worst of all, maybe none of what's happened is about me at all. Because I just don't matter that much. Not to her! Wow, that would be a nightmare, it's probably that.

CARTER. Addison –

ADDISON. Oh sorry also real quick my ex-girlfriend just offered me a job composing music for a film that shoots in California next month, and I should probably take it because like, CAREER! But once she threatened to kill herself if I didn't come over in the middle of the night to help her cut her cat's nails? Anyway I think I'm moving to California in six weeks. So. Yeah...Is that what you wanted me to say?

CARTER. ...*YES.*

ADDISON. Well, there you go! What's the diagnosis doc?

CARTER. We're five minutes over time and I have another client waiting.

> (**ADDISON** *leaps up and throws a thumbs up.*)

ADDISON. Welp! Serves me right for doing the thing again. Haha, see ya next week, sorry I'm like this!!!!

> (*Finger guns that* **ADDISON** *immediately regrets, then* **ADDISON**'s *out.* **CARTER** *stares at the door for an infinite, incredulous beat.*)

> (*Sharp blackout.*)

> (*Sharp lights up on* **CARTER** *sitting on the couch, and* **DOC** *sitting on the armchair.*)

CARTER. It's like this every week, Doctor Dobbs. She comes to my sessions. She deflects, *relentlessly,* for forty minutes. And then in the last five she spews out the craziest – these...stories!

DOC. Does it trouble you?

CARTER. *Yes.*

DOC. Can you identify why?

CARTER. I NEED CLOSURE! It's like a soap opera! I need more episodes!! I don't sleep. I can't sleep anymore – I lie awake, staring at the ceiling, wondering when Addison's co-worker is going to realize she's obviously queer and in love with Addison – and will it be too late when she does?? Because Addison will have already moved to California with her narcissistically abusive movie-producer ex!

DOC. Okay let's...

> (**DOC** *trails off as* **CARTER** *puts her head her in hands and screams a low rumbly scream before confessing:*)

CARTER. And there's something worse – I'm not doing my job. I mean, I don't have to, she doesn't leave me any time to! But I'm *afraid* to do it anyway. I'm afraid I'll say something that will alter the course of her life and it'll get worse and...how do you live with that? Do you ever think about how people just drink up the advice we give? I don't know anything! I'm very stupid and unintuitive actually! Why can't people see that?? They just keep trusting me, it's horrible.

DOC. Your advice is clinical, not personal.

CARTER. I know, I know. And I've never felt this anxiety before, not with any other patient. I just – it's frustrating! She's been seeing me almost a year, why is she still so nervous? Am I horrible at my job?

DOC. It can take a shocking amount of time to earn someone's trust. It's okay if you don't make progress for a while still. And to doubt yourself is normal, but I have no reason to think you're not an excellent therapist.

CARTER. Thank you.

DOC. ...Perhaps you can ask her more leading questions next session?

*(**CARTER** sighs. Sharp blackout. Lights snap back up on **ADDISON** in the hot seat, **CARTER** in the doctor's chair.)*

CARTER. Tell me about your day.

ADDISON. Your...plants are looking...well...

CARTER. How are things with Ruth at work?

ADDISON. Is that a dracaena?

CARTER. Do you still have feelings for her?

ADDISON. Dracaena are very hardy.

CARTER. Addison.

ADDISON. What? I'm complimenting you! Good taste in plants. Practical.

CARTER. Addison.

ADDISON. Ruth and Charlie were making out in MY cubicle on Monday and I found them and it felt like getting STABBED so I guess I freaked out and I maybe shoved Charlie like a LITTLE – just like, *get out of my cubicle you crazy kids!* Haha but I guess it was like, a light sort of assault and so they fired me –

CARTER. *(!!!!!)* Addison!

ADDISON. Right?? And then I met with my ex about the movie and she told me she's still IN LOVE with me even though she'd never said she was in love with me ever BEFORE and I felt. Nothing. And I was going to leave and she was like crying and throwing these potatoes – just like this big bag of Yukon golds one by one – across the apartment and I like – I *caught one*. Like, in my HAND. And it was – it was *funny*. Like you had to be there, it was very funny. And we *laughed*. And I was just like transported back to this time when I loved her so much and she would look at me like I was beautiful and I *was* beautiful, definitely solely because of *how* she looked at me and after the first time we had sex I immediately dropped 'bi' and just called myself a lesbian because I just *knew* it so certainly which is so rare for me and I...so I...we...um...

CARTER. There's nothing to be ashamed of if you slept with her.

ADDISON. I made hash browns.

CARTER. Oh.

ADDISON. – And then I slept with her. Fourteen times over the last three days. I think she lives in my apartment now?

CARTER. We –

ADDISON. I know. I know we're out of time. But also Ruth called me this morning and said she was sorry about what happened with Charlie and that she wanted to talk and so I haven't taken a full breath of air in approximately eight hours or so.

CARTER. Maybe we can start with that at the top of the session next week. At the *top* of the session, Addison.

ADDISON. I'm sorry doc, I'm really sorry.

CARTER. You have nothing to be sorry for, I didn't mean – Therapy is *challenging* –

ADDISON. No. I'm sorry, doc, this is my last session.

> (*The air goes taut.*)

CARTER. (*Trying to maintain professionalism.*) You...have two more sessions. And I didn't think you had decided about the move –?

ADDISON. The production schedule got moved up and Laney's insistent that we throw the few potatoes we got left into the U-Haul this weekend and drive out west for the shoot. I don't feel I can say no. I don't even have a job here now.

CARTER. *(Almost dizzy.)* You...

ADDISON. And this is really hard for me, you know? I don't mean – I mean we both know the situation's INSANE but I mean ending *this*. With you. I know therapy is one-sided and you're a professional and all that. But you've come to feel like a second mom to me or like a cool aunt if that's too much and even though I'm a mess it's really helped having someone to just kind of talk to – even just for five minutes and...um... I'll just...miss you. Ya know?

CARTER. I...

ADDISON. Should we hug goodbye? I mean I would like to. But I understand if it's weird or not allowed.

CARTER. It's –

(An intercom on **CARTER***'s side table buzzes.)*

SECRETARY ON INTERCOM. Your next patient is waiting, doctor, should I send him in?

CARTER. I...

*(***ADDISON** *stands.)*

ADDISON. I'm so sorry, doc. I'll get outta your hair. Thank you so much for everythi –

*(***CARTER** *hits the intercom button.)*

CARTER. Cancel the next appointment.

SECRETARY ON INTERCOM. But –

CARTER. Thank you.

*(***CARTER** *turns the intercom off.)*

Sit down, Addison.

*(***ADDISON** *sits.)*

ADDISON. You didn't have to do that.

CARTER. I know. Listen. You, like most women currently alive on the planet, have low self-esteem. But no matter how those shiny windows distort your reflection, you're not grotesque, you're entirely normal. You are a normal, attractive human being, Addison. Laney is a narcissist. The way she treats you is a clear case of narcissistic abuse, which is characterized by periods of intense idealization of the partner, followed by a rapid discarding of them. She pulls you in when she feels she's losing you, and when she feels you're invested again – when you're attached – it's likely she'll drop you again for the thrill. Ruth is clearly in love with you but deeply uncomfortable with her own sexuality. She probably wants desperately for you to pursue her, but I don't think you should. I certainly don't think you should go to California where Laney will have active control over your finances, your living situation, and virtually every other aspect of your life. Potatoes included.

ADDISON. You're saying...

CARTER. Don't go to California. You were fired, you can collect unemployment here. We have resources to help you find another living arrangement, another job. You deserve someone who loves you fully and treats you well. You deserve that, Addison. You are worthy of kindness and love.

> (**ADDISON** *starts to cry.*)

> (*Blackout.*)

> (*Lights up on* **CARTER** *on the couch and* **DOC** *in the armchair.*)

DOC. You said all that?

CARTER. Yes.

DOC. And she just cried?

CARTER. Yes. But it was cathartic. I think.

DOC. And then?

CARTER. And then we talked for forty-five minutes. And then she left.

DOC. What did she decide?

CARTER. She didn't. I told her I'd keep next week's session open for her. And then we said goodbye like it was...you know, goodbye.

DOC. How do you feel?

CARTER. I haven't taken a full breath of air in three days.

> *(Sharp blackout.)*

> *(Sharp lights up on* **CARTER** *in the armchair and no one on the couch.)*

> *(***CARTER*** stares at it. As if willing* **ADDISON** *to materialize. She does not.)*

> *(***CARTER*** sighs a deep, primal sigh of letting go. She pulls out a vape pen and takes a hit. Mid-inhale,* **ADDISON** *bursts through the door without knocking.)*

ADDISON. WASSUUUUUP!

> *(***CARTER*** jumps, fumbles hiding the vape pen, knocks over a cup of coffee – but she beams once she catches her breath.)*

CARTER. Addison! You came.

ADDISON. Yeah, Doc, I was wondering how you'd feel about...COUPLE'S THERAPY!

> *(***ADDISON*** throws open the door and a woman walks in behind her. The woman

smiles and shakes her head at **ADDISON**'s *theatrics.)*

CARTER. Oh my goodness, is this Ruth?

CASS. Naw, I'm Cass. Fuck Ruth. Fuck Laney too.

(**CASS** *and* **ADDISON** *high-five.)*

CARTER. Well, I like you very much!

CASS. Sorry for the dramatics, Addie wanted to be cute.

ADDISON. I –

CASS. It *was* cute, babe. Very cute.

CARTER. Please don't apologize, it's lovely to meet you.

ADDISON. After our last session I went to a bar to think things over.

CARTER. That seems to have worked for you.

ADDISON. Yes. Cass was the bartender.

CASS. Guilty.

ADDISON. Lucky.

CASS. Very.

CARTER. Why don't you both sit down and tell me all about your week?

CASS. Oh, I don't want to actually intrude on your session. I know she's already ten minutes late –

ADDISON. That's my fault –

CASS. That's no one's fault, babe, that's just life. I'm gonna go wait down at the Starbucks on the corner. Text when you're done, I'll get you that weird sugar monstrosity you like so much.

ADDISON. Thank you.

CASS. It was really nice to meet you, Doctor Carter. She's basically obsessed with you.

> (**CASS** *kisses* **ADDISON** *on the check and then ducks out of the office.* **ADDISON** *is suddenly self-conscious.*)

ADDISON. Sorry, if that was –

CARTER. YOU DID IT!!!!!!

> (**CARTER** *leaps up and hugs* **ADDISON**. **ADDISON** *hugs her back. It's a nice meaningful hug that we invisible spectators are sincerely lucky to view.*)

Sorry, please come, sit down and tell me everything.

> (*They both sit in their usual places.*)

ADDISON. Well, after our last session I needed a drink, but I didn't want to go to my USUAL spots because Laney knows them and could show up – she's like that, honestly, it's INSANE. Anyway I googled some reviews of local dives around this neighborhood, and there was this bar call Roscoe's and the review was: "too much lesbian drama: one star." So that sounded perfect and I went and just started chatting with the cute bartender about what was going on in my life and the cute bartender turned out to be Cass – anyway, I already had the U-Haul with all my stuff in it so Cass just hopped in and we went to her place –

CARTER. (*!!!!!!!!*) You took the U-Haul to *her* –?

ADDISON. I KNOW! So I moved in on uh, Tuesday, and it's been about the best six days of my life, doc, even though I'm a raging lesbian stereotype and not very much else now – but like it's *funny*, so it feels okay? So yeah, I texted Laney that I quit and was not going to California and that I was going to instead block her on everything, and then I blocked her on everything and

Ruth has left me sixteen missed calls this week and I *do* feel something about that but – Sorry, are we out of time?

CARTER. No, it's only been about five minutes since you got here. We have half an hour left at least.

ADDISON. I didn't ask how you were.

CARTER. I know. I'm very proud of you.

ADDISON. How are you?

CARTER. I'm wonderful.

ADDISON. It just feels so one-sided if I...I don't want you to think I don't care about you. Or is that dumb and weird?

CARTER. Therapy is a strange emotional place, Addison, it's normal to feel confused about it, and about our relationship. But as your unofficial, honorary second mom and/or cool aunt, know that I do care about you very much. And also that I obviously don't want to discuss my plants more than wherever this story is leading, okay?

ADDISON. Right, okay. Thank you. This feels like...

CARTER. Progress?

ADDISON. Yes.

CARTER. Yes.

> (*A breath. An exhale of silent yes. Something settles.*)

...So then what happened?

ADDISON. Well, I listened to Ruth's messages. There was even one from boring CHARLIE telling me how torn up Ruth was about the whole thing but I haven't been sure how to reply... (*Is it crazy to want to be friends, or* *try to be friends with her? That's probably impossible and naïve or is it really mature actually? Am I really mature?)*

*(After "reply", **ADDISON**'s voice fades out as the lights do on their conversation.)*

End of Play